FREMONT PUBLIC LIBRARY

W9-BEP-717

PEDRO

PEDRO GOES
TO MARS

by Fran Manushkin

illustrated by
Tammie Lyon

PICTURE WINDOW BOOKS

a capstone

WITHDRAWN

Fremont Public Library
1170 N. Midlothian Road
Mundelein, IL 60060

Pedro is published by Picture Window Books,
an imprint of Capstone.
1710 Roe Crest Drive
North Mankato, Minnesota 56003
www.capstonepub.com

Text © 2021 Fran Manushkin
Illustrations © 2021 Picture Window Books

All rights reserved. No part of this publication may be reproduced in whole or in part, or stored in a retrieval system, or transmitted in any form or by any means, electronic, mechanical, photocopying, recording, or otherwise, without written permission of the publisher.

Library of Congress Cataloging-in-Publication Data is available on the Library of Congress website.
ISBN: 978-1-5158-7081-4 (library binding)
ISBN: 978-1-5158-7315-0 (paperback)
ISBN: 978-1-5158-7083-8 (eBook PDF)

Summary: Pedro would love to take a trip to planet Mars! Are his climbing skills good enough for the planet's rocky surface? Can he pack enough sandwiches to keep himself fed? Will Pedro's big imagination lead him to Mars, or will he decide that Earth is the planet for him?

Designer: Bobbie Nuytten
Design Elements by Shutterstock

Printed and bound in the United States.
PA117

Table of Contents

Chapter 1
Mars Looks Cool

Pedro was reading about

Mars. He told Miss Winkle,

"Mars looks cool. It would be

fun to go there."

Katie raised her hand. "I
nt to go to Saturn. I'll ride
ound on its rings. I'll get
nice and dizzy!"

Miss Winkle said, "You might not like it. The rings of Saturn are made of dust and ice."

"Yikes!" yelled Katie. "I'll go somewhere else."

That night, Pedro told his

dad, "I'd like to go to Mars."

"Are you sure?" asked

Pedro's dad. "It's far away."

"That's okay," said Pedro.

"I have a big suitcase, and I

like long trips."

"Mars is 225 million miles away," said Pedro's dad.

"No problem," said Pedro.

"I'll pack lots of sandwiches."

"And bring some cows for milk," added Pedro's dad.

That night, Pedro dreamed
about going to Mars.

His spaceship was crowded

and noisy. The cows never slept!

Chapter 2
Exploring Planets

The next day, Pedro read

more about Mars.

"It's very rocky," said Miss

Winkle.

"Great!" Pedro smiled.

"I like climbing rocks."

The class read about

Pluto too.

JoJo said, "If I lived on

Pluto, I would see five moons

outside my window."

"Wild!" said Pedro.

Katie told the class, "Saturn has 82 moons."

"No way!" said Pedro.

"It's true," said Miss Winkle.

"That sky is very crowded!"

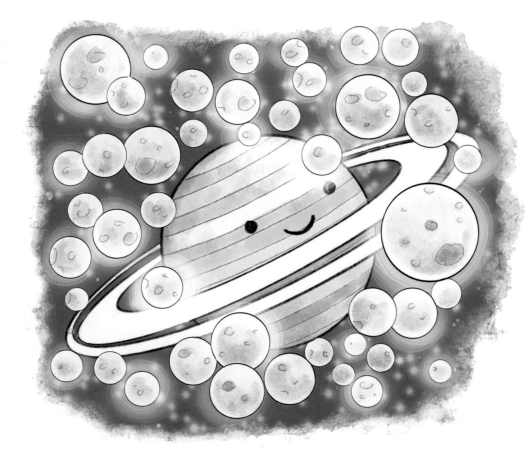

She told the class, "Each of the planets goes around the sun. How many days does it take for Earth to do it?"

Sofia, a new girl, said,

"It takes 365 days."

"Right," said Pedro. "I must

wait 365 days for each new

birthday. That's a long time."

Later, Pedro asked his dad, "How many days does it take Mars to go around the sun?"

His dad looked it up. "It takes 687 days."

Chapter 3
A Very Nice Planet

The next day, Pedro told

Katie, "When I go to Mars,

I will have to wait 687 days

between birthdays."

"Wow!" said Katie. "That's a long time."

"For sure!" said Pedro.

After school, Pedro and

Katie and JoJo played soccer.

The sun was shining, and a red

cardinal sang a happy song.

Pedro said, "Earth is a ver
nice planet. I think I'll sta
here for a while."

"Good idea," said Katie.

That night, Pedro went

to bed, smiling at the moon.

The moon smiled back!

About the Author

Fran Manushkin is the author of Katie Woo, the highly acclaimed fan-favorite early reader series, as well as the popular Pedro series. Her other books include *Happy in Our Skin*, *Baby, Come Out!* and the best-selling board books *Big Girl Panties* and *Big Boy Underpants*. There is a real Katie Woo: Fran's great-niece, but she doesn't get into as much trouble as the Katie in the books. Fran lives in New York City, three blocks from Central Park, where she can often be found bird-watching and daydreaming. She writes at her dining room table, without the help of her naughty cats, Goldy and Chaim.

About the Illustrator

Tammie Lyon began her love for drawing at a young age while sitting at the kitchen table with her dad. She continued her love of art and eventually attended the Columbus College of Art and Design, where she earned a bachelor's degree in fine art. After a brief career as a professional ballet dancer, she decided to devote herself full time to illustration. Today she lives with her husband, Lee, in Cincinnati, Ohio. Her dogs, Gus and Dudley, keep her company as she works in her studio.

Glossary

cardinal (KAR-duh-nuhl)—a songbird with black coloring around the beak and a crest of feathers on its head. The male is bright red.

crowded (KROU-ded)—having a lot of people or items in a small space

dizzy (DIZ-ee)—having a feeling of being unsteady on your feet

noisy (NOI-zee)—loud

planet (PLAN-it)—a large heavenly body that circles the sun

Let's Talk

1. What are some of the reasons that Pedro would like to visit Mars? Would you like to visit Mars? Why or why not?

2. Imagine you are traveling to another planet. What sort of things will you pack for your trip?

3. How does Pedro feel at the end of the story? How do you know?

Let's Write

1. Write a story about traveling in a spaceship with cows.

2. Draw a picture of yourself in outer space. Then write a sentence to describe how you feel to have left Earth.

3. Choose a planet and write down three facts about it. If you don't know three facts, ask a grown-up to help you find some in a book or on the computer.

JOKE AROUND

Why did the cow go to outer space? It wanted to go to the moooooooon!

How do you know when the moon has enough to eat? It's full.

What did Mars say to Saturn? Give me a ring sometime.

How do you throw a birthday party in space? You have to PLAN-et.

WITH PEDRO!

🍁 What do planets like to read? Comet books!

🍁 What do planets like to sing? Nep-tunes

🍁 Where did the astronaut keep her sandwiches? In her launch box

🍁 Why didn't the sun go to college? Because it already had a million degrees!

HAVE MORE FUN WITH PEDRO!

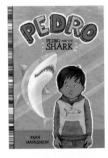

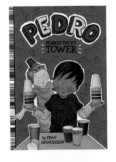